A JOURNEY TO BOSTON

Novels by Mary Ellen Chase

A JOURNEY TO BOSTON

a novel by

MARY ELLEN CHASE

W · W · NORTON & COMPANY · INC · *new york*

Fic
CHA

THIS STORY IS DEDICATED IN GRATITUDE
AND ADMIRATION TO MY MANY FRIENDS OF
POLISH BIRTH IN THE CONNECTICUT VALLEY.

Contents

"I guess no one ever really wants to leave his own country. . . . But America offered us things we couldn't have at home—land that didn't cost much; and work that brought in more money than work at home; and an awful lot of hope for the future. I guess the hope counted for more than the land or the money. I guess hope was the main thing that prodded us on."

one

The
Bright Land

THE WIDE VALLEY of the Connecticut River must be one of the brightest lands in all the world. It is as bright as Florence, or as Fiesole, or as the brown hill towns of Umbria under the hot Italian sun; as bright as Provence even with the added light of the Mediterranean; as bright as the sparkling Spanish islands of Majorca, Minorca, and Ibiza. Perhaps this wide valley is at its brightest in Western Massachusetts, for, as the river broadens there on its way toward the sea, the land broadens also to make room for vast, sunlit fields of tobacco, asparagus, and onions.

People who live in Western Massachusetts, in the old towns of Amherst or Northampton, Hadley or Greenfield, Sunderland, Northfield, or Deerfield, or on the farms which nudge the shoulders of all such towns, are conscious always, at all seasons, of this amazing brightness, whether it is born of the sun during the long, hot summers, or of the incredible brilliance of the autumn colouring, or of the wide, sunswept reaches of snow which mark the slow, reluctant, tarrying winters. Perhaps, indeed, their awareness of it helps more than a little to dispel, or at least to lighten, the long, unintelligible darkness of threescore years and ten.

Not that rain does not fall in this region as it falls elsewhere on the earth. Yet, singularly enough, many of the rains are night rains; and even those of the days are, for the most part, gentle rather than violent, their drops and lines of water sparkling in the air, lingering on and within the thirsty grass, shining in pools upon the roads and pavements. A rare dismal day almost always has its bright moments and usually closes in a clear sunset. The dawns of this Connecticut Valley are bright dawns. The hesitating twilights are bright also.

Lesser gifts of Nature than the sun, the brilliant autumn trees, and the winter snow do their part in adding to this singular brightness. The spring and the summer fields, stretching east and west from the river, unless they have been ploughed and sown, are often bright with buttercups or charlock. The tangled roadsides glow with the yellow of loosestrife, St. John's-wort, and the lesser celandine. Yellow is, in fact, a predominant colour in these regions, a warm rich yellow filled with light.

II

The people themselves do their part in adding to the brightness of their valley. During the summer they grow velvety marigolds in their garden plots; and in the autumn these same gardens show masses of chrysanthemums, mostly in various shades of yellow. Certain tobacco farmers contribute immeasurably to this effect of light and brilliance by their net-covered fields, which from a distance look like shimmering lakes of clear water. Even the long red or gray tobacco barns, with their shuttered sides open to the wind which sways their drying leaves, perhaps because of their grace and symmetry and their ample room for great patches of sunlight to rest upon them, *seem* at least to be a part of this all-pervading, all-embracing brightness. One never looks upon them without wondering with gratitude at the wisdom shown in their length and contour, at the way in which they suit the wide fields where they stand with the hot sun penetrating the long, perpendicular openings in their sides and glowing upon their wooden clapboards.

People serve in other ways to enhance this incomparable brightness. Perhaps the very fact that many of them are Polish does its share. For there is a remarkable vitality in the Polish nature, a strength and a mental agility which have made them lively citizens of their adopted country, eager to do their part toward the common welfare. Apathy, or carelessness, or indifference are traits far removed from the Polish mind and personality at its best. Polish Americans are ambitious for themselves and for their children, experimental and enterprising in their work, generous, outgoing, ardent, alive.

The Polish women wear many-coloured scarves on their heads as they kneel upon the brown soil to set the dark-green tobacco plants in the spring or to cultivate the sharp shoots of the onions as the summer days advance. Such women have a way of moving slowly forward upon their knees. They seldom rise and walk. And, as they work, their bright heads lend brightness to the earth as their mothers' and their grandmothers' heads used to do in the old fields at home.

The men who work on the land along with their women folks do their share also in adding to the brightness of this region and not only through their net-covered tobacco. Many farmers grow pumpkins and squashes among their other crops so that their fields in early autumn glow with the yellows and the oranges of these stout and homely fruits. They pile them, too, in barnyards and on lawns and at roadside vegetable stands. In September and October one never walks or drives through this Connecticut Valley without smiling at these ungainly mounds of squashes and pumpkins heaped in uneven, bulging pyramids on green grass, or against barnyard fences, or under bright trees, or before the doors of farmhouses.

III

This story is, in fact, about a truck-load of green and yellow squashes which had their humble share in freeing the minds and cementing the friendship of two Polish farmers named Tarnowski and Malekski. It may not be the most agreeable of stories, but in its essential features it is an entirely true one, its main incidents having taken place only a few years ago; and whatever darkness it may possess is in stark and sombre contrast to the very brightness of the valley in which these men had lived and laboured for many years.

Tarnowski's Christian name was Jan, a common Polish name; and Malekski's was the familiar Stanislaw, a long-time Polish favourite. The ending *ski* in Polish has the force of the German *von* or the French *de*. Thus Jan Tarnowski means simply Jan, or John, Tarnow, his surname identifying some town or village in which his ancestors had once lived long ago; and

Stanislaw Malekski is, of course, merely Stanley Malek.

Both Jan and Stanley had become proud citizens of the United States; and their children, who looked upon themselves as Americans rather than as Polish, favoured the American form of their surnames. Jan and Stanley had learned to love the Connecticut Valley, which in its farming areas had become largely Polish in the fifty or nearly one hundred years since the first Polish immigrants had come to seek their fortunes far from Poznań and Cracow, Lodz and Warsaw.

Like all Polish people Jan and Stanley venerated the old country; yet, like the thousands who had preceded them, they had learned how to adapt themselves to the new. Unlike their countrymen in the huge industrial Polish settlements of Chicago, Pittsburgh, and Detroit, they themselves still clung, like so many of their forbears, to the soil and counted themselves lucky to wrest a living from the land. It was a good living, too, when compared to what the tired, wornout home fields had offered them when they were young boys dreaming of their American future in Polish villages not far from Warsaw.

Neither was young any longer. John Tarnow was nearly sixty years old and Stanley Malek but a

few months behind him. Both had children and so
many grandchildren that they rarely counted them
except when name-days, or birthdays, or the coming
on of Christmas made such a counting necessary.

two

The
Kitchen

IN THE EARLY MORNING of October 1st, in the
year 1963 (a Tuesday morning as it happened), Stasia
Tarnowski and Helena Malekski were working in
Stasia's kitchen. They were neighbours on adjoining
farms; and, whenever their husbands drove to Boston
with produce, they had formed the habit of spending
the day together in one or the other of their kitchens,
helping each other to catch up on odd, neglected tasks
like washing woodwork or turning out cupboards and
closets, duties perforce postponed by the usual hum-
drum necessities of everyday existence.

Stasia and Helena had risen early on this first day
of October in order to get their men folks off for
Boston in good time. With the new turnpike and
this best of autumn days Jan and Stanislaw would be
in Boston well before noon. Such good and wise
timing would ensure them a fine place in Faneuil

Hall Market where at dawn on Wednesday they could sell their squashes after a restless and perhaps uneasy night in Jan's truck. They would have the afternoon on Tuesday either for wandering around Boston to see its sights or for taking in a movie on Tremont or on Washington Street.

"They'll have a good time," Stasia said to Helena. "Trust those two boys to have a good time, Helena!"

"Yes," Helena said.

She did not at the moment say anything else to Stasia; but she kept on thinking to herself what a good time her Stanislaw would have. It was this genius for having a good time which had made her at last determine thirty-five years ago to cast in her lot with Stanislaw. He somehow always managed to transcend the most ordinary happenings into extraordinary ones, to endow the most trivial of things with excitement and pleasure. Stanislaw really had a genius for converting the most meaningless affairs into matters filled with an odd significance. If he so much as stuffed some feathery asparagus greens into an empty milk bottle, her drab kitchen was suddenly transformed into a garden, rich and strange. If he so much as sat down after supper on the stoop at their back door with his smelly old pipe, the sunset streaming across their fields took on a new splendour. If he so much as said, "A fine supper, Helena," after he had wiped the last shreds of potato and onion from his plate with a piece of her good Polish bread, she felt a new life surging inside her, burying all the burdens and worries of her long day.

She might say only *Yes* to Stasia; yet that necessary, empty monosyllable was in Helena's mind like some brilliant searchlight discovering one by one all those many things which had made her life in this new country comfortable and good.

II

She thought now of this comfort and this goodness not in exact details, but in a general sense of well-being, both physical and emotional, as she and Stasia polished some aluminum pans to a new brightness. In another week or fortnight, when their men drove again to Boston with the remaining squashes, *her* kitchen and *her* sitting-room would be the scene of her and Stasia's work. Her copper, she decided now, would benefit by their scouring. There was nothing in Helena's kitchen which she loved so much as she loved her copper-bottomed saucepans and her skillets, all hanging in a gleaming row from the hooks which Stanislaw had carefully inserted along the edge of a pantry shelf.

"Copper costs money," Stasia had said more than once with more than a shade of disapproval in her voice. "Aluminum looks wonderful to Jan and me after most a lifetime of plain old tin. *We* can't afford pans with copper bottoms."

Who could afford what? Helena asked herself now as she thought of her copper and of the words which Stasia would doubtless say yet again. And just what did *affording* mean? Did it mean only the reckless spending of hard-earned money on unnecessary things? Or did it mean also the capture of new joys, the wonderful even if guilty sense that you owned something a bit out of your class, a bit above your station in life, a bit better than the possessions or even than the desires of your neighbours?

Stanislaw had bought the jaunty, copper-bottomed cooking dishes, the two round, roomy copper-bottomed skillets, one large, the other small, the four saucepans of different sizes, the quite incredible tea-kettle, whose copper bottom curved far up its sides like a band of flame.

"Oh, you shouldn't have, Stan!" she had cried, even while her eyes gleamed and glowed with delight and pride. "You really shouldn't have! Polish folks like us don't rate such marvels!"

"*You* rate everything on earth, Helena!" Stanislaw had said.

He had said it in Polish because, as she knew, he was too embarrassed to use the more definite, less unmistakable English words, which even after years of use still sounded harsh and unfamiliar when one allowed the heart to speak, as, of course, one did only on rare occasions. For this speech of the heart one instinctively returned to the language of one's childhood.

Was there a woman in the whole wide world, Helena had thought then and thought again now in Stasia's kitchen, who could afford *not* to hear a thing like that from her husband, after more than thirty years of marriage, more than thirty years of striving to get ahead on a farm which demanded all one's time, all kinds of new and difficult knowledge, all manner of daring, costly experiments? If there were such a woman in the whole world, she thought, it was not she, Helena Malekski.

III

Stasia Tarnowski and Helena Malekski looked like hundreds of other farm women of Polish extraction—women who, like themselves, had been born in Poland or who, as the children of young Polish couples, had begun their lives in New England, in the thriving tobacco regions of Connecticut and Western Massachusetts. They had the stout shoulders and arms, the large, capable hands, the broad hips, the brown eyes, the unlined, cheerful faces of most of the Polish women of late middle age whom they knew. They were in no sense handsome; yet they looked and were strong, able, and content. They had found life, on the whole, generous and kind and were rarely disposed to complain of its inevitable hardships, its baffling, unsolvable mysteries.

They worked well together now, not getting in each other's way, holding the same standards of efficiency and cleanliness, enjoying the results of their scrubbing, their setting things to rights. When they talked, they spoke in English, using it easily and, because of their children and grandchildren, all of whom had little, if any interest in the language of their ancestors, feeling actually more at home in their use of it. They kept their Polish in readiness, however; for the older people among them still clung to their native speech, knowing no other with any degree of familiarity and deploring the fact that it was surely dying out and quickly, too, even among the original newcomers.

This sure and certain death of the Polish tongue was always bound to be the paramount and uneasy topic at most family gatherings. Nor were the old sparing in their denunciations against their sons and daughters who had allowed such apostasy to rule among their children and their children's children. Perhaps a disquieting sense of guilt prompted Stasia and Helena to talk of the old language now as they worked with their scouring rags and polishing cloths.

"Sometimes I think," Stasia said, "that we should have been more strict with the children. Father Kominski says that. He thinks it's a pity for them not to know any Polish. They can't even follow his sermon for the old people in church. They wriggle, he says, and sometimes look even mocking as he speaks the Polish words. He thinks we've done wrong by them; and perhaps he's right."

"Priests don't know everything," Helena said. "They don't have a lot of children yelling out American words and refusing to answer you when you speak to them in Polish. And, after all, listen to you and me. English comes much easier, even to us who were born in the old country."

"I know," Stasia said. "But it's not just the priests. It's the college professors from all these colleges in this Connecticut Valley. It's other learned people, too. They think it's dead wrong for children to speak only one language. Our Jan was always telling his father and me what his teachers said even when he was just in the primary school. But we couldn't see that it made much difference about the Polish. He just didn't want to speak it, easy as it came to him. We made him speak it, but it was a chore for us, all right. He studied French quick enough, and even German one year, though his father was always telling him how the Polish people at home hated the Germans."

"I know," Helena said in her turn. "We did hate the Germans back in the old days at home. How we did hate those Germans! There was a little German boy at school—Hans, his name was—round and chubby with eyes as blue as forget-me-nots. You must remember him. I'm sure he was a nice little boy; but we all hissed at him and called him pig. *Swiniak*, we yelled all together until we had made him cry. I can just see the big tears rolling down over his round, red cheeks. Then we pointed our fingers at him and went on calling him *świniak* until he cried some more. I'm afraid children are horribly cruel, Stasia."

"Probably," Stasia said. "But that hatred for the Germans was somehow put into us as soon as we were born. I remember how we looked down on men who crossed over to Germany to work in the harvest fields even for a few weeks in the autumn the way they used to do when we were young. My grandfather was always telling us that there were many good Germans and that no country ought to hate another. My grandfather was a good man. He knew a lot of Germans, too, and admired them no end. I often think how sad he would be if he could know that the old hatred has never died."

Helena sprinkled some scouring powder on the bottom of one of Stasia's pans before she spoke. She de-

cided not to say anything more about that ancient
hatred, but instead to ask Stasia a familiar, often-asked
question.

"Do you and Jan ever want to go back home,
Stasia? Do you ever mean to go?"

"I don't know," Stasia said.

She was silent then for several minutes. Helena
was surprised when she began to speak again, for Stasia was seldom communicative and never confidential.

"We talk about it often," Stasia said, "but there
aren't many folks left now who really belong to us,
only two brothers of mine whose very faces I wouldn't
know if they looked in at that doorway there, and
a lot of cousins of us both. Jan isn't so eager about
going as I am, even if we could ever manage the cost.
He says he remembers when he was a boy how folks
came back and how they never seemed to belong any
more. He says they seemed almost like curiosities in
some queer show with their better clothes and their
different voices speaking Polish that was full of mistakes. He says they laughed at the old ways and
bragged a lot about America and about all the com-
forts here. Jan would never brag, of course, but I don't
think he really wants to go back, and it's *things*, not
people, that I'd like to see once more before I die."

"What things?" Helena asked quickly. She could
see by the sudden flush creeping up on Stasia's cheeks

that she was embarrassed by her unusual candour.

"Well," Stasia continued, a bit hesitantly, "I'd like to see the old village street with the strips of land for farming stretching out behind the houses, all fenced or hedged in as they used to be so that everyone could know just what land was his own. I'd like to see if the stained-glass windows in the church look just the same —that one with the red roses wreathed about a crown —how elegant that window always did seem to me! I'd like to gather mushrooms in the forest. I'd like to hold a *zloty* in my hand. I'd like to buy a big loaf of fresh bread from Martula, the baker (they say he's still there baking). And I'd like to see if they still plant potatoes right up to the front doors of the houses."

"As for me," Helena said, emboldened, almost startled by Stasia's wishes which she had not expected to hear, "as for me, I'd like to know if some of the old folks still speak in proverbs the way they used to do, like *Don't get into a wagon without reins in your hands,* or *Guests in the house mean God in the home.* You know. My grandmother now, she was a great one for proverbs. She must have had thousands of proverbs sitting there in her head and waiting to be let out through her mouth."

"Well, I guess we shall never see or hear all those old things," Stasia said. "I'm afraid we're just transplanted Polish folks for good and all, Helena."

"I'm afraid we are," Helena said.

And for the moment she really felt afraid, although of what exactly she didn't know. Nor did she have time to find out. For, just as she was puzzling over her senseless fear, she saw Mrs. Waskiewicz coming up the walk toward Stasia's kitchen door.

IV

Mrs. Waskiewicz had formed the habit of calling when she knew that Jan and Stanislaw had set forth for Boston and that Stasia and Helena were, in consequence, working together. Mrs. Waskiewicz, whose Christain name was Anya, *had* been back home to her native village, which like that of Stasia and Helena was near Warsaw and the Vistula River. She had gone two years earlier with her husband Michael, who had been a neighbour of hers in Poland when both were young; and since her return she had talked of little else. She had found things so odd and unfamiliar that she had felt completely out of place, a stranger in her native land.

"I might as well have been French, or German or even Russian," she had said over and over again until her words had become like the refrain to some old song. "I wasn't Polish any longer. Don't ever go, Stasia. Don't ever go, Helena. Don't ever let Jan and Stanislaw go. There's only heartaches over there after all

those horrid days on the ocean and more on the dirty
and noisy trains. Just don't ever go. Just let's stay
right here for better or for worse. Maybe it's for
worse—I never know—but most times I think it's for
better."

V

Anya Waskiewicz was smaller than most Polish
women. With her slight frame, her narrow shoulders
and hips, her small hands, her rather dainty feet at the
end of thin legs and ankles, she looked as though she
might insinuate herself into any situation she fancied
and without too much notice. Yet notice was the one
human response which Mrs. Waskiewicz craved; and
since she craved it so greedily, she usually managed to
elicit it. She elicited it now from Stasia and Helena in
spite of the fact that they did not especially want to
hear or to talk of a past which had become so dim to
them both that it was almost forgotten, lost irretriev-
ably and not too regretfully among the details of
house-keeping and farming and the ever-increasing
families of their American children.

"It wasn't the big things," Mrs. Waskiewicz said
now, "that—what do the young folks say in English?
—oh, I know—*got me down* back home. Not the big
things, like weddings. There were two weddings while
Michael and I were there. They lasted almost a whole

week with all kinds of goings-on—parties every night
at the tavern, processions with bands, serenades, extra
Masses at the church, much too much vodka, all manner of doings, all sorts of nonsense just as in the old
days when we were young. I was tired out long before
those two weddings were over. 'How they do it, I
don't know,' I said to Michael. Or like the priest calling and having a platter of fried eggs cooked just for
him, no matter what the time of day. 'Father must have
his fried eggs, no matter what,' my sister said. 'If
Father doesn't get his fried eggs, how can we face him
for Confession come Saturday afternoon? One egg
soft, and the other egg turned and hard,' my sister said.
'Not like good old Father Savarski, who always
wanted both his eggs hardly done at all.' No, it wasn't
the big things that I minded. They were just so different from things here that they didn't count any longer.
Even our to-do here about weddings is nothing to that
at home. You can shed big things, I kept on telling
Michael. They're so different that they don't belong
in America at all. It's the little things that you could
have kept alive even in a new country if you'd had a
real mind to. 'Twas those little things that brought an
ache to my throat and tears to my eyes. I got to wishing I had cared enough to keep those little things alive."

"What little things?" Helena asked Mrs. Waskiewicz, whose eyes were beginning again to well with

tears.

Helena tried her utmost to put a note of eager-
ness into her voice largely because she could see that
Stasia did not mean to ask Mrs. Waskiewicz anything
at all. Stasia was almost angrily cleaning her sink, although she had already cleaned it to perfection, Helena
thought. Stasia was clearly hoping that silence would
terminate Mrs. Waskiewicz's stay. But Helena knew
better. She had already discerned something big and
foreboding waiting menacingly behind Mrs. Waskiewicz's preliminaries. Once her purely introductory
comments were out of the way, Helena knew, they
would discover this far bigger matter which was making Mrs. Waskiewicz's heart ache and her eyes brim
with tears, not now in Poland, but in the Connecticut
Valley.

"Just what little things, Anya?" she again asked
Mrs. Waskiewicz, this time with real solicitude in her
voice.

"*Really* little things," Mrs. Waskiewicz said.
"Like braiding flowers and vines and bits of bright
ribbon in one's hair. You remember, Helena, how our
mothers used to plait flowers in our hair for special
days at school or for Saints' Days. So that our braids
had a green leaf here and there, or a buttercup, or a
blue periwinkle. We could have done that here if we'd
really cared to. I could have decked out my Yadwiga's

braids just like that."

"No, you couldn't," Stasia said sharply, looking
at her red, rough hands as she raised them from the
sink. "No, you couldn't have done that, Anya. Yadwiga wouldn't have taken it after one morning at
school or after half an hour at Mass. Don't be silly,
Anya, after all these years. Those things are gone, for
good and all, the little things and the big. Both are
gone. Yadwiga isn't Polish any longer. I'm one of
those who wishes she was Polish, but she just isn't; and
the worst of it is she doesn't *want* to be Polish either.
She wouldn't have let you braid buttercups and peri-
winkles in her hair for half a minute."

"What other little things, Anya?" Helena asked
quickly, surprised that Stasia had spoken and so
sharply. She had again perceived the big matter stew-
ing away in Mrs. Waskiewicz's troubled mind; and
she knew suddenly that it had to do with Yadwiga,
who hated her Polish name and who was called *Wiggy*
for short by all her friends.

"Why, like all the photographs on the walls,"
Mrs. Waskiewicz said. "I wonder just why Polish folks
have such a fondness for photographs. I guess I'd forgotten how they love pictures of folks. I didn't know
who half the likenesses were of, I really didn't. My
sister said she wouldn't wait for the Easter whitewash-
ing to take them down and dust them off. She'd just

make use of me, she said, so I took down all the pictures of all the relatives, and dusted them off, and then
hung them up again. I kept asking her who was this
and who was that. Who was Uncle Karasanski, the
cobbler, and who was Aunt Pepinka, who made such
good apple dumplings though I'd forgotten all about
them, and Cousin Wurtzelo, who married the mayor's
daughter, though even the priest said it would prove a
mistake as it surely did. All the old folks and hundreds
of children, it seemed to me. The children all looked
alike, round and too fat-faced, and decked all out in
furbelows, and fuss. 'Does going to America make one
forget one's own folks?' my sister kept on saying. She
didn't like it for a farthing, I could see that. I mean
my forgetting who folks were.

"No, don't go back home, Helena. Don't go back
home, Stasia. Don't grieve if you never see the Vistula
again. It floods in the spring just as it used to do, and
ruins half the houses in the villages, just the same. And
in the dry seasons it smells of the filth they still throw
into it. The Connecticut used to make me homesick
for the Vistula, but never again, I said to Michael once
we'd got back here to the farm. That's just what I
said to him: *Never again!* He can tell you that's exactly what I said."

Helena suddenly realized what terrible words
Never again were, summary, final, sad, frightening.

Not Anya Waskiewicz's *Never again*, but all the *Never agains* of life. They were just as terrible in Polish as they were in English, Helena thought. She looked at Stasia to see if she, too, had felt the awesome power of those two simple words; but clearly Stasia had not. At least, she was polishing away at the pipes and the faucets above her sink although they already shone quite brightly enough, Helena would have said.

Perhaps the sadness of Mrs. Waskiewicz's two words and the burden lying so heavily in her mind made Helena's next question one of honest concern and friendship—a question born of the quick, warm understanding that Mrs. Waskiewicz really longed to talk and, what was more, needed to talk, desperately needed to unload her burden, whatever it was, to bring it out where it could be looked at, mulled over, shared, and quieted.

VI

"Is Yadwiga really going to college, Anya?" Helena asked. For that Yadwiga was her mother's burden, Helena had not the shadow of a doubt. She could even see Yadwiga's stout Polish frame sitting there solidly among all Mrs. Waskiewicz's fluttering resentments and fears, dominating them all, laughing at them, cruelly pushing them willy nilly, this way and that, out of her own stolid determination to be American rather than Polish.

For a moment Helena longed to gather up Mrs. Waskiewicz in her own strong arms as she might have gathered up some crying child, to pat Mrs. Waskiewicz on the back and say: "There, there! Don't cry. I'm right here." But, of course, she didn't. She merely repeated her question about Yadwiga's going to college.

"That's what we've all been hearing," she finished. "I just thought I'd ask you if it's true."

"No, it isn't true," Mrs. Waskiewicz said. "I wish it was true, but it isn't. Yadwiga did aim at college. For four whole years she aimed. She got the best rank at the Academy—you've surely heard about that—it was even in the paper with a real headline that gave her name, *Yadwiga Waskiewicz*. She was something called a *valedictorian*. She had to write a special address, you remember, for the graduation exercises. It was a good speech, too. We felt really set up, her father and I. Her father was so proud that he cut out the column from the paper and carried it round in his pocket to show folks. Then, after it was most worn through with all his showing, all his hauling of it out and folding it up again, he sent it back home with a sheet of paper which he wrote out in Polish so the folks there couldn't possibly not understand. Even the headline he put into Polish, too. It looked

queer, even to me, with all its z's and t's and k's; and
Yadwiga called him a silly old fool, which made him
really sad, only she didn't care a red cent. Not
Yadwiga! She didn't want that her father should
send her address back home for the folks there to
read, which he did together with the headline and
the notice, even though it took him hours to put the
speech into Polish and not very good Polish either.
And before he was through he had to get the priest
to help him. Yadwiga called him a *blithering idiot.*
Neither of us quite knew just what *blithering* means
in English; but, I take it, it means the worst kind of
idiot."

"I'm sorry she isn't going to college," Helena
said. And she found that she really felt sorry, even
though she didn't much care for Yadwiga, whom
Helena thought brash and ill-mannered. Her regrets
had deeper roots than the future plans of Yadwiga
Waskiewicz. They stemmed from that pride, felt by
the best of the Polish, whatever their station in life,
in the dignity and distinction which learning gives to
a people.

Anya Waskiewicz was not, like Helena, consumed
by any such pride. Instead she was face to face with
personal grief and bitterness.

"I'm sorry, too," she said, her tears becoming
more copious by the moment. "And I'm more sorry for

the reason. You'll hear it soon enough so I may as well tell it to you now. Yadwiga isn't going to college and then teach school as she's planned to do for years and years because she's going to get married."

Stasia stopped her polishing of the pipes at Mrs. Waskiewicz's announcement. She stood still at the sink with the polishing cloth in her hand. The cloth was a piece of red flannel from an old winter shirt of Jan's.

Helena thought suddenly how gay and bright the cloth looked. She felt almost a kind of unreasoning anger against it, as though it were flaunting itself in the face of human sorrow and distress. She was swept again by the absurd desire to gather Mrs. Waskiewicz up in her arms and murmur "There! there!" to her. Instead, she said and did nothing at all. Like Stasia she merely stared at Mrs. Waskiewicz and waited for her to tell them more about Yadwiga.

VII

Mrs. Waskiewicz began to tell them more just as soon as she could manage the tears in her throat. The big round tears—as big and as round as those on the cheeks of the little German boy named Hans, Helena thought—which kept rolling down her thin, anxious face didn't give Mrs. Waskiewicz too much trouble, for she could just wipe those away with her apron; but the ones in her throat kept choking her so that her words trembled and quavered.

If she only wouldn't cry! Helena thought. Still, perhaps Mrs. Waskiewicz's very tears meant that her sorrow was more bearable. Tears often meant just that, Helena had learned over the years. It was the tearless sorrows that were usually the unendurable ones.

"Yes," Mrs. Waskiewicz said. "Yadwiga's getting married at Christmas time, perhaps even before Christmas. We haven't planned on just the day. And she isn't marrying Vladislaw Sladowski as we have hoped all along. Vladislaw has loved Yadwiga almost since they both were born; but he's become just a common lump of Polish earth to her. He doesn't count a red cent any more, even though he's got a tidy sum of money in the savings bank and a nice bit of land all paid for, land enough for a nice new house and at least ten acres of tobacco, Michael says."

Mrs. Waskiewicz paused now in the recital of her news to take some swallows from a cup of coffee which Stasia had placed before her on a small table brought by Helena from the sitting-room for this very purpose. Stasia and Helena stopped their work and drew their chairs up to Mrs. Waskiewicz's table. Coffee in the middle of the morning had become almost a rite with them; and they knew that Anya

Waskiewicz expected her rich, creamy cup, well sweetened with plenty of sugar.

Perhaps she'll go after the coffee, Stasia thought. Perhaps she really will go, and leave us to turn out the sitting-room. Coffee always means sort of the end of visits. What's Yadwiga to us, after all? Stasia thought.

She'll not go, Helena thought. She'll not go until she's rid her aching mind of what makes it ache. She'll not go until she's really told us about Yadwiga. I'll just help her to come to the point, Helena thought.

"Who is it, then, that Yadwiga's getting married to, Anya?" Helena asked Mrs. Waskiewicz.

Mrs. Waskiewicz took another swallow of her coffee and ate a bit of one of Stasia's doughnuts before she answered Helena. Then she said:

"She's marrying a Yankee boy with a Yankee name. Norton's his name, Robert Norton."

"I never so much as heard of him," Stasia said. She spoke sharply, and as though her ignorance of a Yankee boy named Robert Norton might well exterminate him, put him completely out of being.

"Why should you have heard of him?" Mrs. Waskiewicz said. "I'm sure he's never heard of you. He's never known about any of us, for that matter. We're all Polacks to him. That's what he calls us, *Polacks*. He never so much as heard of Yadwiga until

he ran across her at a party somewhere or other a
year ago. Then he never left her for an hour, seems
like. He has a car, and they drove places. He goes to
that Yale College in Connecticut. He aimed to be a
doctor; but now—well, now he's just marrying Yadwiga, and looking for some kind of job, I suppose.
After all, folks have to eat; and there'll be baby clothes
to get. His parents don't take too kindly to his marrying a Polish girl either."

"I don't suppose they do," Helena said, since
the pause made by Mrs. Waskiewicz just here seemed
to demand some sort of remark.

"But then—well, there it is," Mrs. Waskiewicz
said. "At least this Robert Norton boy has some sense
of doing what's right. Even Michael says that. And
Michael would have taken him right on the farm,
with half an interest in it, too. Only this boy doesn't
know the first thing about farming. He hates it as a
matter of fact. He claims he couldn't tell a tobacco
plant from an onion—to save his life, he says."

VIII

Mrs. Waskiewicz's tear-choked words, even without her mention of baby clothes, left no doubt in
Stasia's or in Helena's mind as to just why a Yankee
boy named Robert Norton was giving up Yale college
and his dreams of a dignified future profession to

marry a Polish girl named Yadwiga Waskiewicz. The
reason was old enough in all conscience; yet when it
struck close to home like this, it seemed suddenly
new and especially filled with sorrow. Stasia felt com-
placently thankful that her one son Jan had married a
Polish girl decently and in order, with no baby coming for three whole years. Helena had no son, but,
God be praised, she could rejoice that all her three
daughters had married young Polish farmers and that
all her grandchildren had been born, perhaps too
quickly in terms of wise spaces between them, but at
least as babies ought to be born, the first fully a year
after each daughter's marriage and all the others at
not too unreasonable intervals. There might well be
too many of them. Too many seemed to be the rule
nowadays what with good health and good compan-
ionship and hard work which required relaxation now
and then. Still Helena, God be praised again, had
never been called upon to bear Anya Waskiewicz's
pain and disgrace. She longed again to be of help to
Anya. She said:

"You mustn't grieve too much, Anya. It's just
the way things are, I guess. This Robert Norton boy
and Yadwiga were just out of luck, I'd say. Most
young folks nowadays do things before they're married that we'd have thought wrong when we were
young."

"I still think they're wrong," Stasia said. "And I don't just *think*. I *know* they're wrong."

How can she? Helena thought. How can she make Anya more miserable than she is? Who knows what's wrong, anyhow? Whoever dares to know just what's wrong? I've long ago stopped thinking that I know anything at all about what's right and what's wrong.

She tried to find something in her mind that might comfort Mrs. Waskiewicz, that might ease the sting of Stasia's words; but before she had discovered anything which might help, Stasia spoke again.

"What about the Church?" Stasia asked abruptly and still with a hard sharpness in her tone.

Why bring the Church into this? Helena found herself thinking. Aren't things hard and bitter enough for Anya to bear without the Church and all its rigid, uncompromising rules?

And then she all at once realized that the Church to Stasia and Jan meant something quite different from what it meant to her and Stanislaw. Stasia's son Jan had been an altar-boy in St. Barbara's church nearby almost before he was big enough to light a candle and carry a cruet. Stasia had always, it seemed to Helena, been washing and starching surplices for young Jan to wear as he bowed and knelt and handed all the holy vessels to the priest.

There were all manner of sacred pictures in Stasia's house. Even in her kitchen there was a terrifying one of the Lord showing His bleeding heart. Stasia always blessed herself with the sign of the cross whenever she passed by that certain picture, no matter what she might be doing with pots and pans, meat loaf or cold ham. And in Stasia's sitting-room there were crucifixes on the wall which called for more signs of the cross on Stasia's breast. Sometimes Helena made a sign, too, but only when Stasia was steadily watching her and always, she feared now, out of deference to Stasia rather than to God.

To Helena and Stanislaw the Church was merely the Church, necessary, of course, and an integral part of the old life back home. One always went to Mass as a matter of course, usually early on Sunday to get it done and out of the way, Stanislaw said.

"Now that's over, Helena," Stanislaw often said, "we can have a good long Sunday in rest and peace."

But to Stasia the Church meant God Himself. Stasia and Jan were always on friendly, even intimate terms with the priest, whose cassocks Stasia mended, sponged, and pressed, and for whom she always seemed to be cooking something or other. So to Stasia the question which she put to Mrs. Waskiewicz had much point, cruel as it seemed to Helena. And as though the question were not enough, Stasia completed it with a brisk comment.

"I shouldn't imagine that Father Kominski would be any too happy about such a wedding," Stasia was saying. "I don't take it that this Robert Norton's a Catholic, like Yadwiga?"

Why does Stasia have to be so hard? Helena asked herself again. Sometimes she isn't hard. Sometimes she can talk about mushrooms in the forest and stained glass in the church at home. Why does she have to be so hard with poor Anya?

IX

She felt relieved now to see that Mrs. Waskiewicz was managing a feeble smile through all her tears. Apparently, the Church, which might well have caused an almost insurmountable stumbling-block to the marriage of a Polish girl to a Yankee boy, was causing no stumbling-block at all. Mrs. Waskiewicz seemed almost too eager to make that fact clear. Once she had thanked Stasia for refilling her empty coffee cup, she hastened to explain that religious difficulties in themselves were not adding to her distress.

"No, he's no Catholic," she said, "but he's willing enough to be one. His family are Methodists—I think that's the name—but he says that doesn't count a dime with him. He says he just wants Yadwiga, and he'll take her, Church and all, he says, even though he doesn't think his parents will be too pleased to have him a Catholic. So Father Kominski is giving him what they call *Instructions*, which means, so Michael and I gather, that the wedding can be in the church proper and not just in the chapel.

"Yadwiga's set on real invitations," Mrs. Waskiewicz continued, "and she's paying for them herself out of what she earned this last summer in that shop, where she worked. You'll be getting them once we've decided on the date. They come in double envelopes, it seems. They're engraved, and they say: *Mr. and Mrs. Michael Waskiewicz request the honour of your presence at the marriage of their daughter Yadwiga to Mr. Robert Norton.*"

At this point Mrs. Waskiewicz wiped away more tears before she proceeded with her added information which, Helena knew, contained other painful surprises. For Helena had begun to realize that there was even more in Mrs. Waskiewicz's anxious mind than a wedding to a Yankee boy, proper wedding though it fortunately was to be, in the church rather than in the chapel. She could see that other worries, niggling though they might be in comparison, were deepening the creases in Mrs. Waskiewicz's thin face, making her lips tremble, causing an odd shaking of the skin on the right side of her face, between her nostrils and her chin. Helena did

not like to see Mrs. Waskiewicz's face shaking like
that; and she tried desperately to think of something
to say which might stop the shaking.

"I've never seen invitations like those," she said
at last. "I'm sure they'll be a real treat. My daughters
never had invitations like those. They just wrote notes
to the neighbours and friends. Their father wanted
them to go from house to house like in the old days
at home; but they wouldn't do that. They called that
corny and *old hat*. At least I think that's what they
said. You remember in the old days at home how we
used to go from house to house to ask the people—
bidding visits, we said they were. We used to kneel
down before the very old folks and put our arms
around their knees, and say: 'There's going to be a
wedding in our family, and our mother and father
bid you to the church and to all the merry-makings
for all the week. We do all hope you can come.' You
remember about how we used to do that, don't you,
Anya?"

"Yes, I remember," Mrs. Waskiewicz said. "It
was a long time ago, but I remember, Helena. I remember all those old ways. Sometimes it's sad to
remember them, but I know we must never forget
them. Only, you see, Yadwiga would never be satisfied with *bidding visits* like at home. She's set on
real invitations in their double envelopes. That's the

proper thing to do now, Yadwiga says."

Stasia moved her chair suddenly. It made a sharp, protesting sound as it grated against the wood of the kitchen floor.

"Yadwiga seems to be saying a lot lately," Stasia said. "Just what more is she saying, Anya?"

Mrs. Waskiewicz looked more frightened than ever, Helena thought. The queer shaking in her cheek increased rather than quieted. Finally she said, as though she were apologizing for her every word:

"The trouble is that Yadwiga doesn't like her name. She's never liked it all her life, but now she wants to change it. It seems you can change your name just by going to some office or other and saying what you want your new name to be. I didn't know you could do any such thing, but it's true that you can. Michael has looked into it, and he says it's all true enough. Yadwiga wants her name to be—well, *Dorothy*, or *Victoria*, or even just plain *Mary*—anything but *Yadwiga*, she says. Michael says he never heard of such nonsense; and, of course, there are the folks back home to think about. They get fewer and fewer all the time; but there are some left there still. Whatever would they say if they read a new name for Yadwiga? Even if they can't really read much English, they'd be able to see that her name was different. I know it all seems foolish enough; but it's a heavy load on my mind. Now whatever do you think of such a crazy notion?"

Stasia answered Mrs. Waskiewicz before Helena had had time to straighten out her own confused thoughts and to think of something to say, something kind and gentle which just might quiet that ominous shaking in Mrs. Waskiewicz's face. Stasia spoke now in Polish as though English were unable to carry her displeasure and disapproval.

"I think it's worse than nonsense, Anya," Stasia said. Helena winced as she heard the hard, stern consonants in the Polish words, tones made even more hard by Stasia's disgust and anger. "Nonsense is too soft a word. I think it's just plain wrong; and I hope you and Michael won't hear of it for an instant. Who does Yadwiga think she is anyhow? No matter whether she wants to be or not, she's just a Polish girl from good Polish folks, and her name's a good Polish name. There were once queens in Poland named Yadwiga, I'm told—*queens*, think of that! *Dorothy* is a silly name, and *Victoria* is sillier. And I don't approve of young men who don't care a dime for the church that brought them up, no matter what church it is! I'd say you were headed straight for trouble, Anya Waskiewicz. I wouldn't be in your shoes, not I—no, not for all the money in all the banks in Warsaw. I thank God that my son married a good

Polish girl named Kasia. She wasn't bent on changing *her* name to *Dorothy* or *Victoria*. And she's teaching her children to be proud that their folks came from Poland."

X

"She'll have a hard time, Stasia," Helena heard herself saying.

She had not meant for a moment to dispute Stasia; but the sight of Mrs. Waskiewicz still so shaken and so frail brought the words tumbling out of her mouth. The sight of the day outside their clean and shining windows had its share, too, in hastening her words, for it seemed entirely at variance with sadness and distress.

As noon approached, the very air seemed more filled with brightness. The sun lay upon the harvested tobacco and onion fields, some of them already green with their newly-sprouted cover crops of winter grain. Its warm, even hot rays pierced the long openings in the tobacco barns where the great, flat leaves hung for curing. Helena could smell the sharp, acrid odor of the tobacco. After a few more days of such warm brightness those leaves would bring money into their pockets and purses, money to ensure a calm and plenteous winter with no worry about food for themselves or for their animals. This is a land of plenty,

Helena thought. I don't think I've once seen a hungry
child since I came to this land.

"Kasia will have a mighty hard time, Stasia,"
Helena repeated. "It isn't so easy after three whole
generations to make children proud of an old country
way across the sea. You can talk all you like, but
talk's not enough. Children who were born in America
want to be Americans. They want American names,
and American food, and American ways. Your Kasia
can't change those things, no matter how hard she
tries. You said yourself before Anya came how even
our own children don't want to speak Polish. It's
nothing to them; and it will be less than nothing to
their children. They think it's just some crazy old
tongue; and their children will think it's crazier. And
they're not interested in any ancestors back there in
Europe. They'll never go back to see them, even if
they were there to be seen."

She felt a sudden, strange sadness sweep over
her. It crept into her voice and made her next words
softer in tone.

"Yes, I know it's sad, but I guess it's just the
price you pay when you leave an old country for a
new. In fifty more years, Stasia, there won't be a real
Pole in this whole Connecticut Valley. We'll all be
just Americans. My Stanislaw keeps on saying that;
and he's dead right, whether we like it or not."

"In fifty years," Stasia said, "I won't be here to see how things are; but so long as I am here, I'm not going to be ashamed of where I came from."

"I'm never going to be ashamed either," Helena said. "Don't get me wrong, Stasia. I'm proud of being Polish, too. But I can't help being glad that I never see anyone hungry any more. It used to be so awful to see hungry children with big, begging eyes and more awful to feel hunger in your own stomach when you were little and helpless. It was awful to feel those pains and to know there wasn't so much as a piece of bread to eat. Those days between when the potatoes were planted and when they began to swell and ripen in the hills—so many of those were hungry days even for us who weren't really counted as poor. I'm glad my grandchildren here don't have to know days like that—when only sleep at night would quiet your hunger, but when you often couldn't go to sleep because of it."

Mrs. Waskiewicz's tears were beginning to flow less abundantly, now that hunger and not Yadwiga had become the topic of conversation. The nervous twitching in her face was lessening, too, Helena noted with relief. She even managed to contribute some words on the new subject, once she had blown her nose.

"That's what Michael says, too, Helena," Mrs.

Waskiewicz said. "Whenever the plates at supper
are loaded with potatoes and cottage cheese and
sauerkraut and a bit of meat now and again, Michael
always says we ought to keep on thanking God that
we're never hungry as so many people used to be in
the old country between the planting and the gather-
ing in. Michael says we owe everything in the world
to America and to this valley where we live. He says
he gets prouder all the time to be a farmer right here
in America. He wouldn't go back home to live for
all of Poland. That's what he says, Stasia. *For all of
Poland*, he says.

"And he don't mind Yadwiga's marrying a Yankee boy—I mean really mind so that he's all upset
about it. He says we're all getting mixed up anyway—
the Irish, and the French from Canada, and the Poles,
and the Slovaks, and the Yankees—so why worry, he
says. Sometimes he don't even want to speak in Polish.
I make him speak it because of the old folks about
who don't like to speak in English. And he does his
best, but it's not very good Polish. And when he writes
his letters home, I have to remind him to begin them
with *Praised be Jesus Christ*, the way we used to begin
all our letters. He wouldn't put that down at the start
if I didn't keep on telling him to. He says it's silly
to begin letters like that. And he keeps on saying that
if you choose of your own free will to live in another

country, then you ought to take on the ways of your new home. He says it's only fair to America to take on American ways."

"Maybe," Stasia said. "But someone has to be loyal to the old ways. Our Jan speaks in Polish to his father and me, no matter how he talks to other folks."

"Is it good Polish, Stasia?" Mrs. Waskiewicz asked, a bit tersely, Helena thought.

"Maybe not the very best," Stasia admitted reluctantly. She hurriedly saved herself by a question. "Doesn't Yadwiga speak any Polish at all, Anya?"

"Only a little bit," Mrs Waskiewicz said. "She can say Good morning—*Dzień dobry*—and things like that. But she doesn't much like to. After all, who can blame her? She was taught English in school, and she reads English books all the time. Shakespeare, now. She's a great hand at Shakespeare. Her father says he can't make out so much as a line in Shakespeare's plays, try as hard as he might; and I must say I'm about as bad as he is. I just don't know what Shakespeare was trying to say. But Yadwiga does. And she can quote hundreds of passages, precisely as they are set down in the plays. Robert Norton says he never learned so much Shakespeare as Yadwiga knows, even in that Yale College."

"Shakespeare's in Polish, too," Stasia said.

"Shakespeare's in every language under the sun,

I guess," Helena hastened to say. "Shakespeare belongs to all the world."

It was odd how proud and pleased she felt over such a remark, which sounded learned as well as all-embracing. Such a statement, she thought, might have come right out of a book instead of only out of her, Helena Malekski's, mouth.

She felt immeasurably better now that hunger and Shakespeare seemed to have taken over. And it was a vast relief to see that Mrs. Waskiewicz was not crying any longer. It was probably better, too, in the long run that Yadwiga and her problems had arisen as they had. Mrs. Waskiewicz had unburdened her mind and heart, and she clearly felt relieved in consequence.

Too bad about Yadwiga, of course, Helena thought. Still, people now had a way of forgetting such accidents. In a few years, especially after a church wedding and all, there wouldn't be many who would give the baby's hasty arrival so much as a thought, if only the marriage worked out well as she had no doubt it would. Yadwiga was, after all, a really fine girl; and Yankee boys often made the best of husbands.

XI

Helena again felt pleasantly conscious of the extreme brightness of the day as, after Mrs. Waskiewicz's departure, she walked the short distance homeward at noon. She was conscious, too, perhaps as never before, of the brilliance of the autumn colouring: that red maple, now, in front of their house, which she and Stanislaw had planted twelve years ago in celebration of the last payment on their home; that clump of golden birches across the village green; those red, red vines crawling over that bit of stone wall. She had never grown quite used to the brilliance of New England in September and October. The autumn colouring at home which she vaguely remembered from her childhood had been dull enough in comparison with this rampant pageantry.

There was something uncontrolled in the effect upon one of such splendour. Even in a dying year one looked forward to joys yet unknown, toward gifts and graces of a future yet unimagined, but made possible by plenty and the lack of anxiety.

Who knew what awaited her and Stanislaw now that they had no cares? We might even go to Florida some winter, she thought, or to California, or, just possibly, even to Bermuda. Some people, even no better off than we are, do go to such places just for pleasure. Why not we, too, Stanislaw and I? she asked herself. After all, we have years left to enjoy things. We aren't really old.

The day was so warm and clear that now in her new excitement she planned to eat her luncheon un-

der the trees on their well-kept bit of lawn. Stanislaw
had mowed the lawn yesterday—for the last time before winter, he said.

"We'll be holing in before long now, Helena,"
he had said when he had stopped his work for coffee
and one of her good *ciastka*.

Yet now, on this benign day so filled with warmth
and sun, the thought of snow and cold seemed impossible even to imagine.

Jan and Stanislaw were in Boston now, she
thought, probably walking along Boylston Street toward the Child's there for their dinner.

"There's no place like Child's for good coffee and
a plate of hamburger or sausages," Stanislaw always
said. "Other places cost a sight more without beginning to give you your money's worth. Child's really
does deliver the goods," Stanislaw always said.

It was just possible, Helena thought, as she set a
little table for herself on the lawn, well in view of the
red maple, and returned to her kitchen to prepare her
lunch, that in two weeks she and Stasia might go to
Boston, too, when their men went with the remainder
of the squashes. That would be a major experience if
only it could be brought to pass. To invite themselves
was, of course, unthinkable; but if the hope rested
long and heavily enough in her own mind, it might just
possibly send a notion stealing into that of Stanislaw.

She would entertain it now, she thought, now as she ate her lunch. In her mind she would look at the shop windows in Boston, wonder at the speed on the new turnpike, study the *Boston Herald* for afternoon movie titles and times. She would fill her head now with Boston, nourish her hope, long for the notion to become so lodged in the mind of Stanislaw that he would himself propose their company.

Even Stasia would mellow through a journey to Boston. Stasia would become less hard, more open to new ideas, more grateful to America, through the unfamiliar sights and sounds of the Boston streets, the pigeons on the Common, a nuisance, of course, but friendly, the hurrying throngs of people. Where does each come from? Helena always asked herself. What lies most deeply in the heart of each, recent grief and sorrow or merely the desire for a new pair of shoes? Is this one bothered by too little money, and that one haunted by illness or by the fear of death?

She loved the journey itself: the sense of careless freedom, the sight of blue lakes here and there, the proud way in which Jan or Stanislaw spoke of the fine, safe highway quite as though they themselves had cut it through the land, faced it with gravel and tar. She loved the wind in their faces, the autumn sunlight, the cloudless sky, and the brilliant trees, the oaks still holding their leaves, the red woodbine

rambling in profusion everywhere. She loved the
knowledge that someone not herself would wash their
dinner dishes, stack away their plates on some great
pile of more plates. She could hardly bear the cer-
tainty that, if they all four went, they would stay for
a night in a hotel, she and Stanislaw in a room with
two beds instead of one, with a bell to call a waiter,
usually an elderly man, who would bring them a bed-
time cup of tea, or perhaps to Stan as an almost un-
heard-of treat a bit of whiskey to be poured into an
ice-filled tumbler and drunk slowly with grunts and
groans of complete pleasure.

She loved most of all the dusky drive home at
nightfall on the second day, the gleam of the light she
always left on in the kitchen to welcome them, and the
way Stanislaw always said:

"Well, here we are back again. And there's really
no place like home, now is there?"

Usually he said it in Polish, perhaps, she thought,
because he suddenly realized that homes were the same
throughout the world, whether in old lands or in new,
and that only the language of his childhood could ex-
press his sense of well-being.

XII

Helena was holding the hope and the miracles of
Boston so closely in her mind as she ate her sandwiches

and drank her good, hot tea that she was more surprised than alarmed when the two State policemen
came across the lawn toward her. They came from
Stasia's house next door. They had made their reluctant call upon Stasia before they had come to tell
Helena about Jan and Stanislaw, some unknown little
boy, and the load of squashes.

"Then you wouldn't know anything at all about
that boy?" one of the troopers asked unwillingly,
keeping his eyes fixed on the notebook in his hand.
"We can't fathom out a thing about that boy. Just a
kid he was, thin and white and not more than nine or
ten years old. Not a sign anywheres on him as to who
he might be. And his bike, if it *was* his, all smashed to
bits. We're just stumped about that boy."

"No, I wouldn't know a thing," Helena managed
to say. "Probably someone they just picked up for a
lift. My husband always liked little boys. But I
wouldn't know a thing about this one."

She was not crying at all as she spoke. In some
odd way she did not feel like crying. And it was even
more odd that the thought of the little boy nagged at
her more painfully than did the thought of Stanislaw,
dead, mysteriously killed on a road leading not to
Boston at all, but away from it—on the westward
road which led toward home.

three

The Journey
to Boston

Jan and stanislaw always enjoyed a journey to Boston. When they had been younger men, they had looked upon such a venture as a sign of growing prosperity and success, this carrying and selling of their own produce, this easy familiarity with farmers from as far away as New Hampshire and the western uplands of Maine. Now that they were older and that prosperity was a reality rather than merely a dream, the journey to the Boston market had become an episode rather than an event, without, however, any loss of its enjoyment.

This October journey with squashes did not as a matter of fact mean money to them so much as it meant security and pleasure, the renewing of old acquaintances, the exchange of ideas, talk with farmers, seen only at the market, about winter prospects and plans for spring. There was even irony in the slender price of squashes, what with their weight and size, and in the indisputable fact that most housewives now really preferred, and wisely enough, to use the frozen variety which could be so seasoned that detection from the natural product was well-nigh impossible.

"Why smash and peel and steam great hunks of squash?" Helena asked Stanislaw. "It really doesn't make sense any longer."

And it really didn't, as any sensible person must admit.

II

Still, however small would be their actual intake of cash in the Boston market, however one chose to prepare squash for the table, there was always the carefree journey, the rolling along the new turnpike at sixty miles an hour, the comfortable sense that one's crops were gathered in, one's tobacco drying, one's home paid for, one's bank balance more than adequate for autumn and for winter needs. There was also the stability of long friendship, of hard work, and of a common background, which, familiar as it was, always meant a closeness of association impossible to men from different environments. No Irishman, for example, whether or not he had ever returned to his green island, could have found talk with a Yankee farmer of English background so easy and natural as

Stanley Malek found talk with John Tarnow.

Few beyond themselves would now have known that they were Polish in both birth and blood; but they knew it, and they recognized it with gratitude whenever they found themselves together for an evening or for a considerable drive like this one to Boston. They might speak in English as they usually did; they might look upon themselves as American citizens as they most proudly did look upon themselves; yet their home fields, their small, compact Polish villages, the customs and habits of their boyhood, their early dreams of coming to America, formed an unbreakable bond between them.

They might not want to return home, even for a visit; yet neither could have borne that their homeland should have passed from their memories. It lay in the mind of each, invulnerable, ever-present, and, in an odd way, reassuring, contributive to their sense of well-being. After a manner that neither could have defined, it was like some fertile tract of land which could be depended upon to bring forth an abundant harvest without too much care and tillage.

III

Now as they bowled along toward Boston in the clear October sunlight, they began to talk about the old years at home, the crops they had nurtured and gathered in, the crude methods of farming which they had taken for granted.

"We might have raised tobacco right there at home," Stanley said. "I've often thought about that. The season's long enough with late frosts and all, and the best of markets close at hand. I wonder why no one ever thought of raising tobacco."

"I suppose because old places don't often care about new ways," Jan said.

"That's right," Stanley said. "Old places, old people, too, they don't often think of new ways. They think about a lot of other things, but not so much about new ideas. When you've grown just potatoes for years and years, you keep right on thinking of potatoes, with some oats and barley thrown in for the animals and a bit of bread. It's like the priest with his fried eggs. Like enough he'd welcome them cooked in other ways, but those notions don't hit folks in an old country. They keep on doing as they've always done. Potatoes for the land; fried eggs for the priest; bare feet until the first snow, except for church and sometimes even there. Same old things in the same old ways."

"Sometimes they're good ways," Jan said.

"And some folks say they do a man good," Stanley said. "Give him the feeling that he knows just where he is. I guess they're right about that. Sometimes it's upsetting to take on new ways. I know when I first came to this country, nothing seemed sure or certain. I always knew there was something I hadn't reckoned on that was bound to show up and that I'd have to get used to. Like new fertilizers, say. When you've saved just dung all your life, every scrap from inside every beast, it's queer and sort of disturbing-like to find you can buy even better stuff all ready for you in a bag. If we hadn't come over when we were just boys and ready for anything, I suppose we'd have found things more upsetting, don't you?"

"Maybe," Jan said.

"Like my mother," Stanley went on. "She never really got used to things so she felt to home. Sometimes I'd find her knitting away in her chair by the kitchen window or else just wandering about the yard. I'd see she was crying, with a tear now and then falling on her knitting. 'What's wrong with her?' I'd ask Helena. 'Homesick, I guess,' Helena would say. 'Old folks don't transplant any too good,' Helena would say. And I guess she was right."

"Maybe," Jan said again.

"Helena always claimed that's why my father didn't live too long over here. He didn't fancy machinery instead of animals. He was plain scared of a mowing-machine. He really was. It didn't seem a time-saver to him. It was more like an excuse for not working hard. He wanted a scythe just as he wanted oxen, and just trudging along behind them. He missed crying *Hets, kso, bys* to them and prodding them along with a goad. He wasn't sick at all, my father wasn't. He just died one night, in his bed, asleep. We found him there in the morning, after we hadn't heard him stirring about. We climbed the stairs together, Helena and I, and there he was with a queer sort of smile on his face as though he was glad to go. Maybe we shouldn't have brought our old folks over once we got on our feet and had our own farms. Maybe they'd have been better off with their scythes and their oxen and their bits of fields. I often wonder if they wouldn't have been happier right there at home."

"Maybe," Jan said for the third time. There didn't seem much else to say at the moment; and Jan Tarnow unlike Stanley Malek was not given to talking at any length.

IV

It was Stanislaw who was the talker. He loved to talk at length about the old ways, with Jan as a listener. There they were, those old ways, of not much use now, to be sure, but always there: the long days spent in watching geese or in herding cattle when they were mere boys, eight or nine years old; the way one worked from dawn till dark, taking such work for granted to-

gether with its backaches, its tired, stiff legs; the
occasional Mondays at the nearest market town
where even one's familiar neighbours seemed, in their
best clothes, like strangers; the coming home at night
to a supper of bread and soup, the soup perhaps with
pieces of eel as a special luxury; the catching of eels,
which came up the rivers and streams on the tidal
waters and then stayed there in the lakes and ponds,
their ugly flat heads, their long, writhing bodies, the
smoking of them on metal racks so that with good
luck they would last through the long winters. All
these old customs and habits for some curious reason
made the past stable and dependable, gave one an odd
sense of safety in the present, made one actually glad
that one had known two lands and two lives, an old
and a new.

"I sometimes wonder," Stanley said now as they
approached the signs for Boston although they were
still miles away, "whether we would have come over
if we had known all the hard work it would mean.
I'm almost sure I wouldn't; and I'm more than sure
I wouldn't have had my parents come. I thought then
that I was giving them a new and better life; but I've
thought since then that I was sort of tearing them up
from their roots.

"Sometimes I get remembering how New York
looked—not so many tall buildings as now, of course,

but enough to make me feel queer enough—like any Polish kid who had lost his way and couldn't find it for his very life. God! I was scared! How scared I was! All the English I knew was three words, *God bless you!—Bóg błogosławy was.* The priest taught me those, good old Father Polachek, God rest his soul; but they weren't much good to me; and that's all I had—not a word of English except that *God bless you.* I couldn't say just *God bless you* to all the questions they asked me on that dock. I had this Massachusetts address on a slip of paper which showed where I was bound; but that's all I had, that and those three English words.

"I'll never forget how kind one of those men was to me. 'If you'll just wait a few minutes,' he said, and in Polish, mind you, for he had been born near Cracow, 'I'll take you over to the station and put you on the train for the place you're going to,' he said. And, believe it or not, he did just that through all those streets which would have scared me out of my wits if I'd tried them all alone. I'm not much of a one for praying; but Helena has prayed for that man every night of her life, even though she doesn't know his name any more than I do or whether he's alive or dead. I'd always heard that Americans were kind to strangers; but I never expected one of them would do all that for just a scared Polish boy."

"You've told me that before," Jan said.

"Well, you'll probably hear it again. I always keep thinking about it when I look back on how I came and how I began to work for Borawski at ten dollars a week and a bed in his barn chamber. You worked for Wetsko then, after you got here two months later than me. And we *worked*, too. A day then wasn't any eight hours as you remember. It was nearer eighteen from the first light in the sky until the last cow was stripped and bedded down, and all your bones were sore and stiff. I used to think I had worked hard at home, and God knows I did, but I worked even harder over here. Only here there was money and hope. There wasn't any hope at home, and not much money. When the money began getting thick in my wallet, I didn't mind my bones any longer."

He stretched his legs now with pleasure. Jan was driving the truck so that Stanislaw could sit beside him in comfort, watch the bright trees, think how well he looked in a new pair of slacks, which Helena had pressed for good measure, and a clean blue shirt, think what a lucky man he was.

"'I'd say we'd done rather well for ourselves, Jan," he finished, with a note of pride in his voice.

"Well enough," Jan said.

"And the best things we got for ourselves were Stasia and Helena, new like us, and scared, too, and not afraid to work in someone else's kitchen. They did work, too. Remember how they slaved away for those big American families, how they learned proper table waiting, and new cooking, and how to speak English, and how to make over their clothes to fit American ways. And all for five dollars a week. That was big money then, forty years ago. And now we all live on Easy Street, Number One Easy Street, I'd say. Why don't we give those girls of ours a break two weeks from today? Bring them along? They'd like a journey to Boston. What do you say to that?"

"It's okay by me," Jan said.

"Helena's likely to throw a real fit," Stanley said. "She hasn't had an outing for I don't know when. She'll put a pad right down on her pantry shelf, she will, for writing down what she'll want to buy in Boston. I expect they'll both be mighty pleased to be invited to come with us, don't you?"

"I reckon so," Jan said.

After a long pause, during which Stanley weighed the wisdom of speech and of silence, he said to Jan:

"Whenever I do something nice for Helena, I always feel as if I was maybe doing a bit more toward making things right with her. You see there was a time when I wasn't quite fair to Helena. My head got turned by another girl, and we did things that we hadn't ought to have done. That's years ago and all past and gone now; but I never get it clear out of my head. Helena knew all about it when it happened; but she stuck right by me. And now that it's all over, and I don't want anyone but Helena, I kind of like to give her an extra good time now and then. You see what I mean?"

"Yes," Jan said. "I see all right."

V

They were not far from the turn which led to Route 128 when they saw the little boy. He was lying flat on his back in the grassy section between the roads leading east and west. He was almost unbelievably thin, and his face was white and drawn. His bicycle was only a few feet away from him. Both its tires were flat, Stanley saw, and the boy himself seemed exhausted, plain done in. He could not have been over ten years old; and his pale, anxious face worried Stanley.

"Let's edge over and stop," he said to Jan, "or take the next turn into the road going back. That kid looks sick to me."

Jan waited for two hurrying cars to pass before he drove through the first entrance on the left and reached the long stretch of grass. Then he and Stanley climbed down from the truck and walked toward the little boy.

"Anything wrong, son?" Stanley asked the child. "You look tired. Want a lift? Are you bound for Boston, too?"

The little boy sat up with obvious difficulty. Both men saw that he was close to tears.

"No, I don't want no lift," he said. "I've got a bet with my teacher that I could ride my bike right into Boston. I'm riding straight down Commonwealth Avenue to Arlington Street. There's a cop there, my teacher says, and if he'll just sign this paper I've got in my pocket to prove I made it on my own, I'll get a five dollar bill from my teacher. Five dollars is a big lot of money; and I'll be rested after a bit. No, I don't want no lift, thank you. My teacher, he says I can't make it on my bike. But I can, once I get my wind back. Once I'm okay again, I'll cross over to the right side for Boston. Then I'll blow up my tires and get going again on my way."

"You won't make it on that bike," Stanley said. "It's not just flat tires, son. The front tire's gone for good. That front tire can't just be blown up. It's near to ribbons, and your chain's balled up, too, I'd say. Where do you live, sonny?"

"Stourbridge," the little boy said. "That's a long way back from here."

"Stourbridge!" Stanley said, amazement raising his voice. "You don't mean you've pushed that bike

with your two feet all the way from Stourbridge? No
wonder you look all in."

"I'm not all in," the little boy said. "Once I get
my wind back, I'll be right as rain. Good as new."

"What's your name?" Stanley asked.

"Ramon Skibitski," the little boy said.

"Well, I never!" Stanley said. "Another Pole, on
my word! Maybe you're kin to me. I shouldn't wonder a mite. My mother's name was Skibitski before
she married my father. Now what do you know about
that?"

"I don't pass for Polish," the little boy said. "All
my folks were born over here. We don't call ourselves Polish any longer. We're Americans."

"Don't you speak any Polish then?" Stanley
asked.

"Not a word," the little boy said proudly. "My
mother and dad don't speak it either. They were
both born over here. My mother can't hardly make
out letters that come from her old folks back in Poland if the priest don't help her out. The priest lived
in Warsaw once upon a time, so he knows Polish. Is
it Warsaw I mean? It sounds like Warsaw, this place
of his, but I'm not sure."

"It's Warsaw all right," Stanley said. "Warsaw's
my home town or my nearest one. This fellow, Mr.
Tarnowski, and I both hail from villages near to

Warsaw."

"How do you do, Mr. Tarnowski," the little boy said politely.

"You've been sick to your stomach," Stanley said, for he had discovered the tell-tale signs on the surface of the road. "You're not fit to push that bike all those miles to Boston. Besides, it won't push as you'd find out quick enough. Tell you what, you let me lift that bicycle on these squashes back here, and you get in with Jan and me. Once we get to Boston or maybe in some nearer place, I'll stand you for two new tires and for fixing up the chain; and we'll find someone coming back this way who'll bring you along. Or you can push your bike once it's fit again, only I'd recommend against it. It's too long a trek for a kid like you. Or, of course, you can get that cop on Arlington Street to sign your paper if that's what you want. He won't know the difference once you get down Commonwealth, if you're on your bike. That is, you can do that if we can just get the bike fixed up for you before we hit Boston."

"No, I can't," the little boy said. "I don't tell lies."

"That's right," Stanley said. "There's not much good in telling lies. They're bound to creep up on you in the end."

The little boy's face grew suddenly whiter. In

another moment he was sick again, retching painfully and at last vomiting into the road, toward which he had staggered across the strip of grass. Stanley held him by the shoulders, and, when he was over his sickness, laid him carefully down.

"I don't think any of us will try for Boston right now," Stanley said. "I think we'll just get you back home. Stourbridge is a powerful long way for a bike, but it's nothing for a car. Tell you what, we'll fix up your bike for you in Boston or some nearer place and bring it back to your house when we come home tomorrow. It will be as good as new, I promise you; and you can try your stunt again some day when you feel more rugged-like. What you need now is to get home and go to bed, with your mother to keep an eye on you. You've had about all you can take, if you ask me."

"All right," the little boy said. "Only my mother's not likely to be at home. She went off this morning before I started out for Boston."

"Where to?" Stanley asked.

"I wouldn't know," the little boy said. "She's always going off some place or other. I don't often know where she goes."

"Does she go off alone?" Jan asked the little boy.

He spoke sharply and suddenly, startling both Stanley and the child. Perhaps he was thinking of his own son, and of how Stasia had never gone off some place or other when their son was a little boy.

"No," the boy said. "She doesn't go alone. There are men that I don't know who come for her; and I don't know where they go."

He may well have noticed the look which Jan Tarnowski gave to Stanislaw Malekski, for his pale face flushed with colour, and he said almost fiercely to them both:

"But my mother's good to me. You mustn't think she isn't kind and good, even if she does go away. If she knew I was sick, she'd stay right to home. You mustn't get any wrong notions about my mother."

"We wouldn't think of any wrong notions," Stanley said. "We're not the kind of men who think wrong notions about mothers. We both had mothers, and now we've got wives who are mothers, too. Maybe your bed's at home if your mother isn't; and that's the place for you right now. Jan and I'll have you home in no time if you'll just show us the way. That's why we crossed over to the road leading back. And you can just tell that teacher of yours for me that he's crazy to let a kid like you make any such bet. Isn't this a school day anyhow? What about school?"

"He let me off," the little boy said. "I'm so far ahead of my class that he let me off for a day. He said I didn't need to come, so that's why I set out for

Boston. He said Tuesday would be a good day without any traffic to speak of."

"Turnpikes always mean traffic," Jan said gruffly. "Bundle him up, Stan, and we'll get going back to this Stourbridge place."

VI

Stanley lifted the little boy in his arms, wondering as he did so how any child no matter how young could weigh so little. He's nothing but skin and bones, Stanley thought. He can't possibly weigh over forty or fifty pounds.

They all three sat in the front seat of the truck, and the bicycle was sprawled across the green and yellow squashes in the back. Stanley continued to hold the little boy in his arms, arranging him across his knees with the crook of his left arm as a pillow for the child's head.

"Now don't you mind being sick again, sonny," he said. "It won't matter a mite. My wife put some extra clean handkerchiefs in my pants' pockets when we set out this morning. So we're all set. Just you be sick whenever it comes on you."

"I don't think I'll be sick any longer," the little boy said. "All I feel now is sort of tired and sleepy. Only I'm sorry I didn't win my bet. I was aiming a lot at that five dollars. I've never had five dollars of my very own in all my life."

"What was you aiming at buying with it?" Stanley asked.

He thought a bit uncomfortably that he ought to be doing his share at driving, only he found it hard to imagine Jan's holding the little boy. Moreover, he was feeling an almost strange sense of acute pleasure over the child's head on his arm and his thin, bare legs stretched out across his knees. He could not, in fact, recall such pleasure in holding any one of his several tough, vigorous grandsons, who were rarely still, and never white, or trembling, or sick.

"Books," the little boy said. "I was aiming at buying perhaps two books with all that money. My teacher can buy books at a cheaper cost just because he teaches school, he says. He said he could buy two books for me with all that money. Only I don't expect he thought he'd ever have to spend it on books for me. I guess he knew all along that I'd never make Boston on my bike."

"Where's your father?" Jan asked, suddenly again and breaking another long silence. "Or haven't you got any father?"

"I had one once," the little boy said, "but he cleared out years ago when I was five or so. I wouldn't know where he is now. He wasn't much good, my mother says. He liked books too much, she says. He was always reading, she says, instead of working like other men. My mother doesn't much like my always reading books."

"Never mind that," Stanley said, for he saw that the child was again near to tears. "All good men read books. You're a real reader, I take it. You like books?"

"Yes," the little boy said. "I've got four books of my own; and if I could get just two more, I could make a nice little shelf for them next to my bed, and have a real library of my very own. I've got a book called *Little Men*, which is rather silly in places, more for girls than boys, I'd say, and a better one called *Huckleberry Finn*, and a really nice one called *The Secret Garden*, and my favourite one called *Captains Courageous*. And I was aiming to buy two more which I've read times already from the library in Stourbridge. They're called *Treasure Island* and *Kidnapped*. They're wonderful books. I'd like them for my very own, so I could read them whenever I had the mind."

"Well, I never!" Stanley said. "You're on the way to being a real scholar, I take it, with all those books right in your head."

He opened the window a trifle wider and saw to his relief that a trace of colour was beginning to creep into the child's white face.

"I aim to write books myself when I'm a man," the little boy said. And then, as though he were ashamed at confessing his dream to two strangers, he hurriedly asked a question on his own.

"What's this country Poland like, do you know? In my geography book it's sort of a brown place with letters that say *The Republic of Poland*."

"That's what it is," Stanley said. "It's a republic like the United States of America. But it wasn't always a republic. In the old days it had kings and queens. It's been badly treated by other countries, Poland has, cut up and taken possession of; but now that's all past and gone, and it's on its own and doing fine, I take it."

"I'm glad," the little boy said. "I didn't mean I didn't like being Polish. I just meant that all the boys I know don't think of being Polish or French or anything else. We think we're all just Americans, and that's what our teacher tells us we ought to think."

VII

Stanley shifted the little boy to a more comfortable position before he spoke.

"I haven't too high an estimate of that teacher fellow of yours," he said. "First, he lets a kid like you start for Boston on a bike in poor shape. To bike to Boston from where you live would be a tough chore for a grown man, let alone a boy like you. And then he wants you to forget where your folks hailed from. We're all Americans. Mr. Tarnowski here and I are American citizens and proud to be; we cast our votes just as all good Americans do; but we don't forget the land we came from. We're proud of Poland. It's a fine country, and it's given some great people to the world, musicians and writers and such-like. You'll learn about them when you grow up. And then you'll feel proud of Poland, too."

"Have you ever been back to see Poland?" the little boy asked.

"No, we haven't," Jan said.

"But we keep it inside us just the same," Stanley said. "It's right there—the place we came from, our mother country, if you know what that means. Some folks want to forget the country they came from; but we're not that kind. And I think you ought to feel proud like us. You tell that teacher fellow what I say. Can you remember that—to tell him?"

"I'll try," the little boy said. "And I'll surely tell him how good you were to me and my bike."

"Maybe you wouldn't know," Stanley said, "but Polish boys were always taught to be kind and help-ful to strangers in trouble. It's a kind of law in Poland to be helpful to folks in trouble, especially if they are strange to you. It's not written down, of course, in books like real laws; but it's a kind of law inside you, if you know what I mean. My grandmother back there near Warsaw when I was about your age used to make me repeat after her: *Don't ever leave a man alone when he needs company*. That's what's called a Polish proverb, and in Poland a proverb is almost like a law. Do you suppose you can remember that to tell your mother and that teacher fellow?"

"I'll try," the little boy said again. "And I'm sure I can remember. I'm very good at remembering nice things like that. But you haven't yet told me what this Poland place is like. I'd really like to know."

"Well, it's hard to tell just from memory," Stanley said. "But there's some things I've never forgotten about it. It's not a country of high mountains like, say, Switzerland; but it's got a lot of nice quiet fields and plenty of rivers. The biggest river is called the Vistula River. That's near where we were born, Mr. Tarnowski and I."

"I've heard of that river," the little boy said. "I'm sure it's in my geography book."

"I'm sure it is," Stanley said. "It's a very important river. And now when you see it in your geography book, you'll know it belongs, after a fashion, to you."

"Yes, I will," the little boy said. "Tell me some more about that country of Poland."

"Well, no one in Poland forgets to say *thank you*. That's another law that isn't written down, but that everybody knows. In Polish the word for thank you is *spasibo*, thank you. How old are you, sonny, anyway?"

"I'm nine," the little boy said.

"Well, if you were nine in Poland," Stanley said, "you'd look after the geese, and once you were older, you'd look after cattle or sheep. That's what all boys your age do in Poland."

"I wouldn't mind doing that," the little boy said. "I like animals."

"Well, if you lived in Poland," Stanley said, "you'd like them even more. Because in Poland folks believe that animals can talk to each other the way people talk. When I was just a boy like you, my folks told me how animals talk, especially at night. A cow will say to another cow, 'Are your folks kind to you? Do they milk you gently, so it never hurts you?' And the other cow will tell her friend all about the folks that own her and how they treat her. That's why in Poland there's a sort of law about being kind to animals. People in Poland don't like to kill animals, even snakes or frogs. There's a saying there, *Don't kill any creature. All creatures also praise our Lord Jesus.*"

"I never heard about that before," the little boy said. "I like that. Did you and Mr. Tarnowski live in Poland when you were young like me?"

"Yes, we did," Stanley said. "We looked after

geese, too, just as I told you, and then, as we grew older, we looked after the sheep and cattle. But we began to think about coming to America when we weren't much older than you are now. We came when we were sixteen years old; but we thought about coming for years before that."

"Why did you want to come so much?" the little boy asked. "If Poland is such a nice country, why did you want to leave it?"

Stanley thought for some time before he answered the little boy's questions.

"We didn't really want to leave it," he said then, slowly and carefully. "I guess no one ever really wants to leave his own country. I get homesick even now for the white mushrooms that used to spring up in the woods after a rain and for the blue forget-me-nots that grew by all the little streams. But America offered us things we couldn't have at home—land that didn't cost much; and work that brought in more money than work at home; and an awful lot of hope for the future. I guess the hope counted for more than the land or the money. I guess hope was the main thing that prodded us on. Do you know what hope is, sonny?"

"Yes," the little boy said. "I know all about hope. I hope I'll grow big and brown and strong like most of the other boys I know. I hope that some day I can run without getting tired and eat a great deal without getting sick to my stomach, and push my bike to Boston without losing my wind. And, most of all, I hope that some day I'll have all the books I want—all standing on a shelf of my own. I shall call that shelf my library. My library is what I hope for most."

"Well, that's a big order of hope," Stanley said, looking at the child's white and prematurely old face. Suddenly he tightened his hold upon the little boy's shoulders and upon his bony, scrawny knees. "That's a big order all right, but I've no doubt you'll get all those hopes. Anyhow, it's hope that keeps us all going on, looking for this and that and not being afraid to work for our hopes until they come true. That's what Mr. Tarnowski and I did, once we came to this country. We kept on hoping and hoping and working and working and saving our money until now we have our two farms all paid for. They're our very own now."

"I'm glad," the little boy said. "I sure am glad that America has been kind to you."

"America's the land of hope," Stanley said, perhaps more to himself than to the little boy. "When I came over here years ago—more than forty years ago, it was—there was an old rabbi on the ship, and he kept saying that to me. *America's the land of hope,* that old rabbi kept saying over and over. Would you know what a rabbi might be, sonny?"

"He's a kind of Jew priest, isn't he?" the little boy said.

"That's right," Stanley said. "That's not a bad way to put it, I'd say. Well, this old rabbi had come from Poland, too, years back. Cracow was his home place, where he had been born and raised. Cracow's a very old city in Poland. It has a great university that is centuries old. All Polish people are proud of the city of Cracow. Sometimes they call it the City of Learning, and sometimes the City of Light."

"Is that the same thing?" the little boy asked. "I mean do light and learning mean the same thing?"

"I reckon so," Stanley said. "I'm not a learned man myself, you understand; but I have a deep respect for men who are. I know they've written books all through the ages so that we can't ever forget about history or such-like things. If you aim to write books as you said a time back, you'll probably some day be a learned man yourself."

"Perhaps," the little boy said. "Anyhow, my mother aims to send me to college. Sometimes she says that's all I'm good for—to read books and to go to college."

He looked up then at Stanley; and Stanley saw to his sorrow that the child's blue eyes were slowly filling with tears.

"But I'm sure she's satisfied with you just as you are," Stanley said, and as he spoke, he held the little boy even more tightly. "Mothers have a way of liking to have their children just as they are. I'll bet your mother's proud of you just as you are. I wouldn't want to be any different if I was you. I'd just go on reading books and aiming to write them some day. It's a fine thing to write books for other folks to read and think about. Just what is it you aim to write books about when you grow up?"

"I'm not quite sure yet," the little boy said. "I'd like to write about trees and flowers, and maybe about rivers, too. I'd like to travel to faraway countries and write about the trees and flowers and rivers in those places. Whenever I look at my geography book, I get to wishing I could some day go to all those countries—to Germany, and Italy, and France, and England—and to Poland, too, now that you've told me what a fine country it is."

"Well, I'd keep right on wishing," Stanley said. "It's wishing like that that keeps a fellow going on and on and makes him want to do his best. Wishing don't cost a cent; and it keeps a man alive in his head, and in his heart, too, if you know what I mean. I've wished for things all my life long, and I intend to keep right on wishing."

"What about you, Mr. Tarnowski?" the little

boy asked.

"Jan's a wishing man, too," Stanley said before Jan got around to answering the little boy. "He don't say much—he's a sort of silent man, as you see—but he's a wishing one, and he's a man full of hopes, just like you and me."

"That's good," the little boy said. "I sure am glad I fell in with two—gentlemen like you two."

VIII

It was the last thing he ever said. For just at that moment the tire of the right front wheel of the truck blew. Just at that moment Jan was driving the truck at a good speed along the western road leading back toward Stourbridge. There was no fence there, only a deep drop-off, so that there was not even a frail obstacle to lessen their fall.

When the State troopers finally reached the place, all three, Jan, Stanislaw, and the little boy, were dead. Stanislaw, one of the officers gathered, had apparently tried to throw the child to one side in order to save him; but the heavy squashes had done their work well. He was quite buried beneath them. Whether they had suffocated him or simply killed him by their weight, it was not possible to say. It was quite clear anyhow that he had not had enough life to weather them or the deep drop the truck had made when it turned over.

Jan and Stanislaw were so messed up in the smashed machinery that it was equally impossible to say just what had caused their deaths. All that was too clear was that all three of them were dead.

four

Stourbridge

Stasia thought it was quite unnecessary for Helena to go to Stourbridge to see Ramon Skibitski's mother. It was kind, of course, Stasia said; yet so really needless that to Stasia, at least, it seemed extraordinary and even a bit absurd. But once things were over, once Jan and Stanislaw had been buried in the earth of their adoption, and the police by every means of detection had discovered who the little boy had been and where he had lived, Helena was determined on her journey.

"Whatever for?" Stasia asked her. "Who's that boy to you, or to me, for that matter? We don't so much as know who he was or why our men folks picked him up. We'll likely never know that, so what's he or his mother to us?"

"Maybe nothing," Helena said. "I just want to go, that's all."

II

She went, on a brilliant October afternoon, just a week from the day that had marked the fatal journey to Boston. It was another day as bright in its sunlight and colour as the first, even now less than a full week gone, had been. She drove the old car which, after ten years of hard service, she and Stanislaw had planned to turn in that very autumn toward a new model. It will do well enough for me, Helena thought, as she drove over the unfamiliar roads toward Stourbridge. I shan't need a new car now. Besides, I like driving this one. We've had good times in this old car.

She could not have said why she drove to the village library to ask about Ramon Skibitski instead of to the post-office or to the general store; but it proved a happy choice. The librarian, a tall, gaunt woman, who in her appearance at least looked quite foreign to the manifold and mellowing influence of books, knew all about the little boy and seemed glad to talk about him.

"He was always reading," she told Helena. "He was a great child for books. He never seemed to get enough of books and reading. He used to stay right here for hours before he took his books home, just bending over books and encyclopedias. Seems like he

couldn't get his fill of maps or of words on paper.
He told me once that he planned when he grew up to
travel to all manner of places. He said he wanted to
see for himself the fields of tulips in Holland and
just what the Alps looked like. He even aimed at the
pyramids of Egypt. He felt sure that some day he'd
see a pyramid for himself. He was such a thin, pale
little boy. I asked him once when he had learned to
read, but he couldn't tell me. He said he couldn't
remember a time when he didn't know how to read.
He was always polite, too, with all his shyness. When
I heard he'd been killed like that, I couldn't believe
it. Did you know him, perhaps?"

"No," Helena told her. "I didn't know him at
all. You see, it was my husband he was with. My
husband was killed, too."

"Oh, I'm sorry," the embarrassed librarian said.
"Well, that little boy lived right down this street, in
the small white house on the right-hand side of the
road just before you get to the bridge over the stream.
I hope his mother's there. Folks say she runs about
too much; but she's a very nice woman, and she sure
set a lot of store by that little boy. She aimed high
for him, I understand, college and all that; and I'm
sure he'd have made her very proud of him. It's hard
to see why some things happen the way they do, now
isn't it?"

"It's more than hard," Helena said. "It's impossible."

III

Before she had so much as seen Ramon Skibitski's mother, Helena began to understand why she had come to Stourbridge. Things suddenly began to take on new reality to her among these Berkshire hills, which blazed with incredible colour under the October sunlight. Out of the thick gray haze in which the events of the past week had hidden themselves, they suddenly emerged, sharp and sombre enough, but at least real and tangible.

Stanislaw was dead. There was no doubt whatever about that. She would never again get breakfast for him; or sleep beside him at night; or reckon their bank balance with him on the first of every month, listen to him fuming over the column of figures; or take pleasure in cooking some surprise for his supper; or just think how wonderful it was merely to live with him.

Here in this sprawling, nondescript small town there was a woman who had lost a son, a little boy hardly ten years old. One did not easily think of such little boys as dead. They lived and climbed trees, collected stamps, filled their pockets with everything under the sun, forgot to wipe their feet on door-mats, made sling-shots and hurled stones from them. The pain of the knowledge that this little boy would never again do any of these things caused pain to nag at Helena, who oddly enough welcomed it in place of numbness and unreality.

Ramon Skibitski's mother was at home in the small white house by the bridge over the stream. She was a young woman, hardly more than thirty years old at most. She was tall and thin with widely spaced brown eyes and a rich colour in her cheeks. How lovely she is to look at, Helena thought. And how clean her house is! This kitchen now—it's far cleaner and tidier than my own.

She was glad to see Helena. She said:

"You were good to come to see me. After all, you didn't know my son, and you've lost your husband."

"I suppose that's why I came," Helena said. "I think my husband must have taken a fancy to your little boy. The way I see it, I think my husband must have been bringing your little boy home. Perhaps he was sick, and my husband thought he ought to be here at home with you. Stanislaw—that was my husband's name—was always fond of little boys. He was always sad that we never had one of our own. We had three daughters, only no sons. But we have nice grandsons. Three of them are about the age of your little boy. How old was he anyhow?"

"Nine," Mrs. Skibitski said. "Just nine. He had his birthday only two weeks ago. I let him have a party and made a cake for him. Only he didn't much care for parties and cakes. He was a queer youngster. I don't think I ever quite made him out—I mean understood just what kind of a boy he was."

As she paused and fell silent, Helena found herself grieving for that lack of understanding. It, in its own dark way, she thought, is another sort of death and perhaps more difficult to bear than merely the cessation of physical life.

Then Mrs. Skibitski said:

"I hope your daughters are good to you."

"They're wonderful," Helena said. "They are always begging me to come and live with them, and they've begged harder in just these last few days. But I've decided I'd rather make out on my own."

Mrs. Skibitski was silent for so long a time that Helena found herself ill at ease, embarrassed, more uncomfortable than she could remember, searching in her confused mind for something else, anything else which she could say. Then the little boy's mother broke her long silence.

"I'm wondering just how one does make out, all alone like this," she said.

"I don't quite know," Helena said. "Only I know

we have to manage it somehow. I guess work's the
answer, especially if you can feel it's work that
counts for other people. Anyhow I'm going to make
a try at it. I've discovered that most Polish folks like
us set a great store by neat rooms and tidy houses,
like yours here for instance. So I'm just going to clean
houses for those who own them and who don't have
time to keep them tidy. I've gathered that there are
lots of people who want women to clean up their
houses good and proper, once a week, say. So that's
what I aim to do. I'm going to be just a cleaning
woman, but the best one I can make myself into.
Sometimes, I've discovered, your hands can make
your heart feel less broken into bits. What about you?
What are you aiming to do? We've got to do something, you know, not just live with our sorrows."

"I think maybe my husband's coming back to
live with me," the little boy's mother said. "He came
back when he knew that Ramon was killed. He loved
Ramon. He loved him so much that all our differences,
his and mine, seemed to fade away like, when he came
back. If he should come back to live with me again,
I'd have enough to do just by making a really nice
home for him and for all his books."

"Did your little boy love books like his father?"
Helena asked. She felt almost a terror in her question.
She thought suddenly that she could not bear that a

love for books had been killed, too, when the truck turned over.

"Yes, he did," Ramon's mother said. "Seems like he was born with a love of books somewhere deep inside him. He never seemed really happy unless he had a book in his hand. He used to stroke his books the way other boys stroke dogs that they love. He'd move his hands over their covers and turn their pages as though even the pages were sort of holy to him. And he always went to sleep with some book in his hand. Whenever I went into his room to put out his light and to see that the covers were over him, there he'd lie with a book in his hand or maybe with his cheek pressed hard against it. 'Twas foolish of me, but I always felt like crying when I saw him like that. He was so thin and so little to care so much for all those words in all those books."

IV

"He was like his father in all that, you understand. Not a bit like me. I can only read and write and not too well either. I've always been almost scared of books; but perhaps I could learn to feel different about them if I had them around me all the time the way I used to have. I never used to think I could miss the sight of a book, but I really do miss them. Did your husband like books, too?"

"Not in any great way," Helena said. "He was just a plain farming man himself. But he always respected men who did. He was often saying that we should all honour men who learn and study and teach. Some plain folks like us laugh at learned men, at all their peculiar ways; but my husband never did. He always felt worried if our grandsons complained about school. He wished he had had years more of school, he used to tell them. Perhaps he and your little boy were talking about books as they drove along."

"That's more than likely," Mrs. Skibitski said. "My son was always talking about books. He started out for Boston on his bike so that he could win a wager with the schoolmaster and get five dollars to buy two more books of his own. I shouldn't have let him go all that long way. He wasn't strong enough to pedal his bike all those miles. His father says that. His father thinks I should have known better than to let him go. I'm afraid his father sort of blames me for Ramon's death. And maybe he's right. Maybe I am to blame."

She burst into tears then, sobbing such dry, staccato sobs that Helena was distressed beyond words. She found herself putting her arms around Mrs. Skibitski, patting her on the back, and saying "There! There!" to her, as a few days before she had felt like doing to Anya Waskiewicz, whose troubles now seemed as nothing to Helena.

Mrs. Skibitski did not take long to pull herself together.

"How kind and good you are!" she said to Helena. "What about Mrs.—is it Tarnowski? What about her? How's she going to make out?"

"She's going to live with her son," Helena said. "She thinks I'm crazy just to keep my own house and go out to work for folks. She says, What are one's children for if not to help their parents? But I know generations don't mix too well. I want my daughters to run their own homes without me sitting around and sometimes perhaps not being able to keep my own thoughts to myself." And then, as though to change the subject and get on safer ground, she asked Mrs. Skibitski about herself.

"Were you born in Poland, then?" she asked.

"No," Mrs. Skibitski said. "I wasn't born there, but my folks were. My father was born near Cracow, and my mother not far from Warsaw. Zewski, that was my name. My father and mother met on the ship coming over; and I guess their fear of a new country sort of brought them together as you might say. Anyhow they got married once they reached New York. Then they came right here to Massachusetts and started to work the way all Polish folks did in those days. My father worked on the tobacco just as a hired man, and my mother worked by the day in American families for folks who needed help. They worked hard, too. I used to see my mother so tired at night that she could hardly get my father's supper. But she never complained. She used to tell me it was wonderful to work for the sake of those you loved.

"I've never myself thought one way or another about being Polish, but my folks did. They loved the old country. That's what they always called it—*the old country*—and it always stayed right there in their minds, like some sort of pleasant dream. I'd say they fared pretty slim over there; but it was always home to them. I've seen tears come into my mother's eyes when she so much as said *the old country*. My folks are both dead now, so I'm all alone as you might say."

"I was born in Poland, too," Helena said. "In a village near Warsaw."

"Well, imagine that," Mrs. Skibitski said. "Do you remember much about it? You're not old. You must have been young when you came over here."

"I was," Helena said. "I was only around seventeen when I came. And I don't remember too much, I'm afraid. My husband was a great one for remembering things back home. He always wanted that we should grow forget-me-nots in our bit of flower garden because they made him think of how they looked in Poland. I don't remember about forget-me-nots, but he did. And he always liked to see mushrooms springing up after a rain, because he used to gather them when he was a boy at home.

"I do remember, though, how kind everyone was to everybody else in that village where I was born. Whenever bad luck hit somebody else, no matter who, seems like people couldn't do enough to help. Once, I remember, a farmer lost some sheep from some disease or other; and the priest went right through the village collecting coins to buy him some more sheep. Everyone gave something—you couldn't think of not giving something, no matter how hard put to it you were yourself. I remember how the priest had a pocket in his cassock, how he kept on clinking the coins there, and how he said: 'You're giving this to God, you know, not just to Peter Walinski, and someday God will do something nice for you.'"

"I sometimes wonder about God," Mrs. Skibitski said, her voice breaking. "He has queer ways of doing things, I'd say. Maybe He needed your husband, but I can't see what use He'd make of just a puny little boy like Ramon, can you?"

"I don't suppose we're expected to know about God's ideas and ways," Helena said. "But I'm sure Ramon isn't puny any longer. I'm sure he's strong and well."

"That's just what his father claimed," Mrs. Skibitski said. "I guess that's what made me decide I'd

better go back to him. When he said that about Ramon,
I guess I even thought I could love him again the way
I did years ago."

She suddenly put her hands over those of Helena.
They were shaking. Helena held them closely in her
own hands until they were quiet. Once they were
still and the clock on the kitchen mantel-piece had
struck three sharp tones, Mrs. Skibitski began to speak
again. Her words were as clear and definite as the
striking of the clock had been.

"You don't know about me," she said, "but
there's something I have to tell you. I'm not supposed
to be a good woman, you see. No one in this town
thinks I'm worth much of anything; but I'd like you
to know that I'm not really a bad lot. Maybe I run
around too much; but that's only because I get lone-
some-like and want company. I've never been untrue
to my husband the way most folks say I have. You've
come way out here just to see me, and I'd like you to
believe that I'm not really a bad lot. I'd never, never
claim that I deserved a son like Ramon was—I'm sure
I didn't—but I'm not bad. I'm just ordinary, and stu-
pid-like, and given to gadding about. I'm sure you're
a better woman than I am, but maybe you know my
sort. We're not bad, only just not good, like you."

"I'm not good," Helena said. "I've never been
very good. My husband used to say he never felt at

home with too good people. 'Let's not be too good, Helena,' he used to say. 'Let's just be decent and kind, so God can use us. I'm sure He can't use people who are too much like Him.' I always loved my husband when he said that.

"And I came to see you just because I wanted to come, and because I thought your grief was greater than mine. My husband had lived a long life as lives go. He was happy, too; he'd done well with things. But your little boy hadn't really begun to live. I felt so bad about him that I thought I must come and tell you so. I feel a great sorrow about your little boy."

Mrs. Skibitski went to her stove from the chair where she had been sitting opposite Helena and moved a saucepan away from the heat.

"You were good to come," she said to Helena. "I have the notion that you know an awful lot about things folks ought to do. Do you think I'd best live with my husband again, try harder to make a go of it once more? He'd like it, he told me when he came a few days back; but I'd hate to make a mess of it as I did before. Maybe you could tell me what I'd better do."

"No one can say what anyone else ought to do," Helena said. "And I guess everyone makes mistakes, or messes as you call them, at some time or other. I know I've made enough of them, and I was very happy with my husband even though just now it seems as if I'd always remember all the wrong and stupid mistakes I made. I can't say what you ought to do; but if I was you, I'd try again, even with all the chance of messes and mistakes. Yes, I'm sure I'd try again if I had the chance."

"I think I will," Mrs. Skibitski said. "I think I'll write to my husband and say I'm ready to try again."

"And after you write your letter," Helena said, "why don't you drive back home to my house and stay right along with me for a bit of a spell until I start out on my cleaning of other folks' houses? Your husband can come to my house to fetch you and bring you back here."

"You don't really mean that, do you?" the little boy's mother asked. "Please don't say it if you don't mean it, because I'd sure like to come."

"Well, get your bits and pieces together right now," Helena said. "I'll just wait outside in the sunlight till you've written your letter and are good and ready. I was so sure you might like to come that I made your bed up before I set out for Stourbridge— with my best sheets, too. And it's a real nice bed."

Then she started for the door and the sunlight outside; but she stopped for a moment at the entrance.

"As I see it," she said, "two folks like us who aim at making brand new lives for themselves can do with a bit of planning. And it can be helpful all around if they can somehow manage to plan things together."

V

When Helena and the little boy's mother started out from Stourbridge toward the Connecticut Valley and the wide, shorn tobacco fields, the land was bright with the brightness of the October afternoon. Helena felt even a strange brightness within herself. This can't be happiness, she thought. I'll never be really happy again. But anyhow it's the absence of pain.

Of course, she could not know that an ancient philosopher had once described happiness in just those words.